This book belongs to

_____

_____

_____

For God, who gave me such a delightful character to write about; my friend Natalie Provenzano-Brodie and my husband, Desmond Finbarr Nolan, who both listened to Mrs. McGee's escapades until their ears burned; and for my dad, Alvin, who opened up dozens of coconuts lickety-split for me when I was a kid – A.Z.N.

For Gill – P.C.

tiger tales

an imprint of ME Media, LLC
202 Old Ridgefield Road, Wilton, CT 06897
First U.S. edition 2009
Text copyright © 2009 Allia Zobel Nolan
Illustrations copyright © 2009 Peter Cottrill
CIP data is available
Hardcover ISBN-13: 978-1-58925-079-6
Hardcover ISBN-10: 1-58925-079-6
Paperback ISBN-13: 978-1-58925-414-5
Paperback ISBN-10: 1-58925-414-7
Printed in China

1 3 5 7 9 10 8 6 4 2

Mrs. McGee's Coconut

by Allia Zobel Nolan
Illustrated by Peter Cottrill

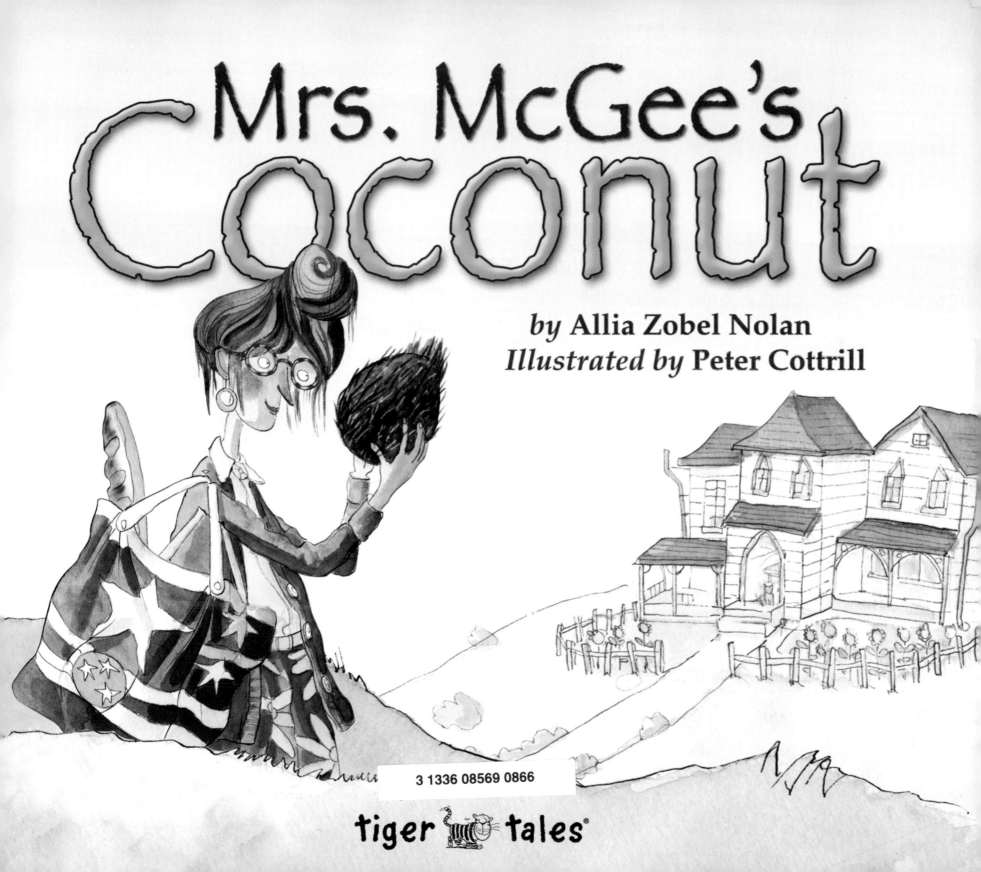

tiger tales

There once was a lady named Mrs. McGee,
who purchased a coconut in Tennessee.
"I'll open it for you," the grocery man said.
"No, thanks," said the Mrs. "I'll do it instead."

"Come look!" said the cat to her good friend, the mouse,
when Mrs. McGee had returned to the house.
The Mrs. was **WHACKING** something on the floor.
She **TH-WHACKED** it so hard that it . . .

ROLLED out the door.

The coconut gathered up speed as it went.
It **BOUNCED**, and it **LEAPT** straight on into a tent.
There, ladies were nibbling rum cake and ice cream.
When they saw the coconut, boy, did they **SCREAM!**

They jumped from their seats, and they ran outside fast.
They peered at this hairy thing as it flew past.
The coconut flattened a cat named O'Mally,
then **THUNDERED** on into . . .

the town's bowling alley.

It spun down a lane, hitting pins for a ... STRIKE! ...then sailed out the door...

onto a motorbike.

Of course, it was driven by Mrs. McGee.
When she saw the coconut, she yelled, "YIPPEEEE!"
But on the way home, she hit bumps in the road.
You guessed it. . . .

The Mrs. lost her precious load.

The coconut **RACED** down a hill toward a tree;
waiting there with a shovel, stood Mrs. McGee.
She swung at the coconut as it whirled by.
But she missed, and then let out . . .

a TERRIBLE cry.

ARRRGH!

A black-and-white dog chased it down to the pier.
It **DROPPED** in a ship . . .

on its way to **KASHMIR.**

The coconut **BOUNDED** from ship to the shore
on an island with lizards and parrots galore.

A smart monkey grabbed it.
And wouldn't you know?
He climbed up a tree and then . . .

DROPPED it below.

SPLAT!

The coconut opened and, wow, what a treat!
The animals gathered and had some to eat.

Meanwhile ... Mrs. McGee bought some walnuts, and well ...

Now, that is a **WHOLE** other story to tell.

The Very Ugly Bug
by Liz Pichon
ISBN-13: 978-1-58925-404-6
ISBN-10: 1-58925-404-X

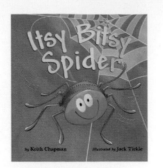

Itsy Bitsy Spider
by Keith Chapman
Illustrated by Jack Tickle
ISBN-13: 978-1-58925-407-7
ISBN-10: 1-58925-407-4

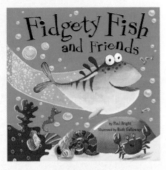

Fidgety Fish and Friends
by Paul Bright
Illustrated by Ruth Galloway
ISBN-13: 978-1-58925-409-1
ISBN-10: 1-58925-409-0

I've Seen Santa!
by David Bedford
Illustrated by Tim Warnes
ISBN-13: 978-1-58925-411-4
ISBN-10: 1-58925-411-2

Explore the world of tiger tales!

More fun-filled and exciting stories await you!
Look for these titles and more at your local library or bookstore.
And have fun reading!

tiger tales

202 Old Ridgefield Road, Wilton, CT 06897

Good Night, Sleep Tight!
by Claire Freedman
Illustrated by Rory Tyger
ISBN-13: 978-1-58925-405-3
ISBN-10: 1-58925-405-8

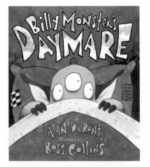

Billy Monster's Daymare
by Alan Durant
Illustrated by Ross Collins
ISBN-13: 978-1-58925-412-1
ISBN-10: 1-58925-412-0

A Very Special Hug
by Steve Smallman
Illustrated by Tim Warnes
ISBN-13: 978-1-58925-410-7
ISBN-10: 1-58925-410-4

Just for You!
by Christine Leeson
Illustrated by Andy Ellis
ISBN-13: 978-1-58925-408-4
ISBN-10: 1-58925-408-2